W9-BYT-237

By Lisa Pliscou

Dude

Fun with Dude and Betty

Illustrated by Tom Dunne

HARPER
An Imprint of HarperCollinsPublishers

For my son, Max

—L.P.

To Katy and Mae

—T.D.

Dude: Fun with Dude and Betty
Text copyright © 2011 by Lisa Pliscou. Illustrations copyright © 2011 by Tom Dunne.
Like, all rights are totally reserved. Manufactured in China.

To get even more dialed in, send a snail mail to HarperCollins Children's Books, an epic division
of HarperCollins Publishers, 10 East 53rd Street, New York, NY 10022, which is a city where
you totally cannot surf. Bummer!

Library of Congress Cataloging-in-Publication Data is available.
ISBN 978-0-06-175690-0 (trade bdg.)

Typography by Dana Fritts
11 12 13 14 15   SCP   10 9 8 7 6 5 4 3 2 1   ❖   This is a most excellent first edition.
www.harpercollinschildrens.com
Mahalo.

I'm stoked to be a member of the Surfrider Foundation,

a grassroots organization that's working hard to protect our

oceans, waves and beaches. Check it out at www.surfrider.org.

~~~~~

With epic thanks to

Christian Puffer

Trevor Cralle, author of THE SURFIN'ARY

Mark Rauscher, Assistant Environmental Director, the Surfrider Foundation

Joe Freeman of Old Soul Surfboards

and my ultra-cool editor, Maria Modugno.

—L.P.

Here is Dude.

Hey, Dude. What's up?

Dude is a way cool guy.

Here is Dude's friend, Betty.

Betty is a righteous surf bunny.

She does *not* live in the Valley.

Look!

Here comes Dude's dog, Bud.

Bud is a most excellent dog.

Good boy, Bud!

Dude and Betty take Bud to the beach.

Look at Bud catch the Frisbee!

Awesome catch, Bud!

Yowza!

Stokaboka!

Check out those waves!

The waves are big.

Surf's up, Dude!

It is cranking today.

See Dude surf.

Whoa!

Look at Dude surf.

Surf, Dude, surf.

See Betty soak up rays.

What a totally rad tan, Betty.

Here comes a gnarly wave.

It is super gnarly.

Oh, oh!

Dude gets biffed by a wave.

Dude wipes out.

Dude and Betty go to the taco stand.

Betty wants the nachos.

Dude wants a bodacious burrito.

What about Bud?

He is hungry, too.

Oh, no.

Dude is out of cash.

No food for you, Bud.

Bummer!

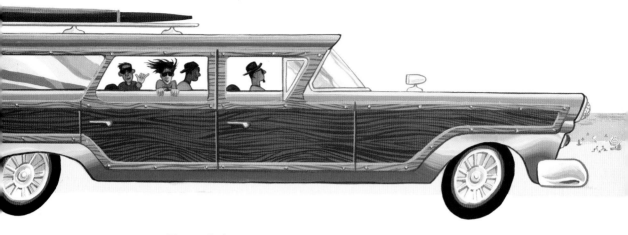

Look!

Oh, look!

A cruisemobile is driving past.

Dude scopes out the cruisemobile.

What a stylin' surf wagon!

It is a total surf bomb.

It is going fast.

Later!

Uh oh.

Bud has chowed Dude's burrito.

Most heinous, Bud!

Bud is harshing on Dude's mellow.

Wait.

It's cool!

Betty shares her nachos.

What a non-bogus babe Betty is.

Dude and Betty leave the beach.

Dude wishes *he* had a stylin' cruisemobile.

Look!

Here is Dude's house.

Dude and Betty go inside.

Dude shows Betty his new Surf Punks CD.

Betty boogies.

She does the surfer stomp.

Dude plays air guitar.

Ta-*weeeee!*

Bud barks.

Oh, look!

Look!

Here come Dude's mom and dad.

"Dude," says Father,

"have you cleaned your room?"

"Dude," says Mother,

"have you done your homework?"

Oh, oh!

What a gnarly scene.

It is time to bail.

Bail, Dude, bail!

Dude and Betty go back to the beach.

Waves are happening.

Dude is stoked.

GLOSSARY

Air guitar. When you pretend to play an electric guitar.

Awesome. Great; fantastic.

Bail. Get out of a bad situation; leave.

Biffed. Smacked.

Bodacious. Amazing.

Boogies (verb form)**.** Dances.

Bummer. A bad experience.

Chowed. Eaten.

Cool. Really great. Hip. Okay (as in "Things are fine now").

Cranking. When describing waves: favorable, great.

Cruisemobile. A station wagon just right for carrying surfboards.

Excellent. Great; cool.

Gnarly. When describing waves: big and very tough to surf. In a general sense, describes something really bad or difficult.

Harshing on [someone's] mellow. Putting someone in a bad mood.

Heinous. Terrible; awful.

Later. As in "See you later."

Non-bogus. Cool.

Rad. Short for *radical*, meaning totally great.

Righteous. Something really good; great.

Scopes out. Checks out; surveys.

Soak up rays. Lay out; get a suntan.

Stokaboka. A happy surfer's shout. See also *yowza*.

Stoked. Really, really happy.

Stylin'. Very cool.

Surf bomb. A cool surfer's car.

Surf bunny. A girl who may or may not be a surfer; either way, she hangs out with surfers.

Surf Punks. A funny surfer band from Malibu, California.

Surf wagon. See *cruisemobile.*

Surfer stomp. A dance popular among surfers.

Surf's up. The surfing conditions are good.

Valley, the. An uncool place far away from the beach.

What's up? What's happening, what's going on?

Wipes out. Falls off a surfboard.

Yowza. A happy surfer's shout.

Lisa Pliscou grew up in California and on the beaches of Mexico where, during a good storm, the ocean would come flowing into the backyard. Which the kids thought was very cool, although the grownups probably didn't. Lisa is an editor as well as a writer, and is the author of five other books, including the novel HIGHER EDUCATION. She lives in the metropolitan New York area with her family. She totally loves Manhattan, but the beach is still one of her most very favorite places on earth.

Tom Dunne is an artist who is based in North Carolina. His illustrations have appeared in *Muse* magazine, and he likes to draw green sea turtles. This is his first picture book.

www.lisapliscou.com
www.tomdunneart.com

For exclusive information on
your favorite authors and artists,
visit www.authortracker.com.